D0645986

WELCOME TO
PASSPORT TO READING
A beginning reader's ticket to a brand-new world!

Every book in this program is designed to build read-along and read-alone skills, level by level, through engaging and enriching stories. As the reader turns each page, he or she will become more confident with new vocabulary, sight words, and comprehension.

These PASSPORT TO READING levels will help you choose the perfect book for every reader.

READING TOGETHER
Read short words in simple sentence structures together to begin a reader's journey.

READING OUT LOUD
Encourage developing readers to sound out words in more complex stories with simple vocabulary.

READING INDEPENDENTLY
Newly independent readers gain confidence reading more complex sentences with higher word counts.

READY TO READ MORE
Readers prepare for chapter books with fewer illustrations and longer paragraphs.

This book features sight words from the educator-supported Dolch Sight Word List. Readers will become more familiar with these commonly used vocabulary words, increasing reading speed and fluency.

For more information, please visit www.passporttoreadingbooks.com, where each reader can add stamps to a personalized passport while traveling through story after story!

Enjoy the journey!

Little, Brown and Company

Hachette Book Group
237 Park Avenue, New York, NY 10017
Visit our website at www.lb-kids.com

Little, Brown and Company is a division of Hachette Book Group, Inc.
The Little, Brown name and logo are trademarks of Hachette Book Group, Inc.

The publisher is not responsible for websites (or their content) that are not owned by the publisher.

First Edition: November 2011

ISBN 978-0-316-18575-2

10 9 8 7 6 5 4 3 2 1

CW

Printed in the United States of America

★ THE ADVENTURES OF ★
TINTIN

THE MYSTERY OF THE MISSING WALLETS

Adapted by Kirsten Mayer

Screenplay by Steven Moffat
and Edgar Wright & Joe Cornish

Based on The Adventures of Tintin series by Hergé

Little, Brown and Company
New York ★ Boston

Attention, Tintin fans!
Can you find these items in this book?

WALLET

CANE

BOWLER HAT

Tintin and his dog, Snowy,

like to find clues and solve crimes.

They work with the police all the time.

Tintin works with a pair of policemen
named Thomson and Thompson.
They look alike, but they are not twins.
They are not even brothers.

Thomson and Thompson visit Tintin
and tell him about a criminal on the loose.
"A pickpocket," explains Thompson.
"He has no idea what is coming!"

"What do you mean?" asks Tintin.

Thomson holds open his coat.

"Go on. Take my wallet," he tells the boy.

Tintin takes the wallet

out of Thomson's pocket.

The wallet snaps right back!

The wallet is attached to the coat with

"Very resourceful," says Tintin.

"Simply childish," says Thomson.

"Childishly simple," corrects Thompso

The policemen tip their bowler hats to

and take off down the street into the f

"I expect he is miles away by now," says Thomson.

"The pickpocket?" his partner asks.

Thomson nods.

An older gentleman walks toward
Thomson and Thompson.
He is the pickpocket!
As he brushes past them,
he slides his hand into Thomson's pocket.

He grabs the wallet and walks away,
but the pickpocket is yanked back
by the elastic!
"I have got you now!" yells Thomson.

The pickpocket lets go.
The wallet snaps back
into Thomson's face.

Thompson grabs the criminal's jacket.
He calls out, "Stop in the name of the law!"
But the thief shrugs out of the jacket
and flips it over Thompson's head.
Thompson stumbles into a lamppost,
tripping up Thomson, too!

Tintin and Snowy hear the shouting.

Snowy growls.

"What's going on?" asks Tintin.

"Come on, Snowy."

They rush down the street
and bump into an older man
hurrying the other way!
"I beg your pardon, sir,"
says the stranger.

Tintin and Snowy find
the policemen on the ground.
"The pickpocket is getting away!"
yells Thomson.
Tintin realizes that he bumped
into the criminal!
He checks his pocket. Snowy barks.

"My wallet is gone!" cries Tintin.
"I have to get it back!"
"You will," says Thompson.
"Leave it to the professionals."

The next day, Thomson and Thompson pay a visit to a man at his home. "Mr. Silk?" asks Thompson.

"We pulled a jacket off a thief," explains Thomson,

"and your wallet was inside."

Silk is the thief, but they do not recognize him!

They return the wallet.

"That is my wallet," admits Silk.

"It must have been stolen from you," says Thompson.

"May we come in?" asks Thomson.

"Oh, no need to come in!" says Silk.

"We insist!" says Thomson.

The policemen follow Silk.
Inside Silk's apartment,
the shelves are filled with wallets!
"Good grief! What is all this?"
asks Thompson.

"It is my collection," says Silk.
"It started with coin purses.
I cannot help it."

"You want to be careful," says Thompson.

"There is a pickpocket loose!

A master criminal! A wallet-lifting thief!"

"I am not a bad man!" protests Silk.

Thompson finds a wallet on the shelf.
"Look at this! It says *Thompson* on it!"
Thomson holds up another wallet.
"No, it is *Thomson* without a *p*,
as in the word *psychic*."

"You have it wrong," says Thompson.

"There is a *p* in *psychic*."

"I am not your sidekick," argues Thomson, not hearing his friend clearly. "You are mine."

"I met you first," says Thompson.

"No, you did not," says Thomson.

"Yes, I did," says Thompson.

"Did not!" "Did!" "Did not!"

The thief breaks down.

"I cannot stand it anymore!" he tells them.

"I will come quietly."

Silk fills their arms with wallets.

"Take them all!" he shouts.

"Good heavens," says Thomson.

"This wallet looks familiar. Is it?"

"It is!" agrees Thompson. "Tintin!"

Thomson and Thompson solve the mystery,
and they return Tintin's wallet right away.
Thompson smiles at their friend and says,
"It is right here in the paper.
That pocket picker has picked his last pocket!"